Lie Like

Trump

The Greatest Guide Ever

For Fibbing, Fabricating

&

other Arts of Lying

Taj Mahal & Marco Ejevarilla

This is a work of fiction, parody and expressive speech.

First Printing, 2018

ISBN 978-1-7327589-0-2 (Color paperback)
ISBN 978-1-7327589-1-9 (Black & White paperback)
ISBN 978-1-7327589-3-3 (Ebook)

Boffo Books
3334 E Coast Hwy
Suite 337
Corona del Mar, CA 92625

www.boffobooks.com

Cover and illustrations by Bianca Pardue

Contents

Lie, n

A **lie** is a statement used intentionally for the purpose of deception. The practice of communicating lies is called lying, and a person who communicates a lie may be termed a

liar.

An act or instance of lying; a false statement made with intent to deceive; a criminal falsehood.

transf. Something grossly deceptive; <u>an imposture</u>.

Introduction

Half a truth is often a great lie.

- Benjamin Franklin

The premise for *Lie Like Trump* can be based on a definition of lying offered by Thomas L. Carson, Professor of Philosophy at Loyola University Chicago in which he's written: "To lie, on (sic) my view, is to invite others to trust and rely on what one says by warranting its truth and, at the same time, to betray that trust by making a false statement that one does not believe to be true." As of this printing, the *Washington Post* has suggested Donald Trump has made over 5000 lies; *CNN* has calculated he's made over 3000 lies in his first 466 days, while the *New York Times* didn't compute a number, but they've included every lie he's made since becoming President. Regardless of the correct number, what is patently obvious is the 45th President of the United States is a pathological liar.

Though lying can have enormous consequences on a pedestrian level, lying by the President of the United States can have catastrophic consequences not only for a President, but for humanity in general. But this isn't a book on the moral and ethical consequences of lying and deception. NO, this is a book focused on the beneficial side of lying and, in particular, how *To Lie Like Trump.* But implicit in the act of lying is also the act of obscuring the truth. In other words, avoiding a question or a topic. This technique has become known in political circles as pivoting, and it's exploited by Democrats and Republicans alike; however, in addition to outright lying, Trump has also become a master at pivoting.

Some may think lying like Trump would be a difficult thing to do given the ease with which Trump so easily allows lies of any type to roll off his tongue seemingly floating in the air and, like oxygen itself, inhaled by humans all over the planet. The Reader may be asking, "How can I, a mere mortal, learn the ways of lying, the fundamentals of which were established as early as Genesis, polished by one of the greatest liars and pivoters in human history and make them work for me?" Do not fear. The answer is near.

A Very Brief History of the Lie

"Yo, Eve," said the serpent. "What's up?"

"Nothing. Just chilling in the garden."

"So, Eve, did God really say you shouldn't eat from any tree in the garden?"

"No, just one."

"Which one?"

"The one in the middle. He said I shouldn't eat or touch it?"

"Wow. Why not?"

"If I did, I would certainly die."

"Really? God said that?"

"Yes."

"What a jokester."

"What do you mean?"

"You won't die. He just doesn't want you to be like him."

"What do you mean?"

"If you eat it, then you'd know as much as he does and he doesn't like the competition. He thinks he's the only one who can fix things. Believe me."

"The fruit does look good."

"Go on, take a bite. How much can a bite hurt?"

Which she did and that bit of deceit was the "first lie." One could even categorize it as the first "whopper" ever told. Of course, the serpent was really the Devil and it's common knowledge the Devil is a liar, is the Father of all lies. He uses words as weapons to lure and deceive his victims…Biblically speaking, that would be as good a place as any to start talking about the history of the lie. And if the Devil is the Father of lies one might ask what was the first lie? Clearly, one could make the argument it was when he said to woman, "You won't die." Of course, we know the Devil, being the Devil, wasn't going to show up as the Devil since that would blow his cover so he came as a serpent. Such a deceitful Devil. Lied about his appearance, lied about immortality. Bad Devil. Gave a bad name to all those serpents that followed. But we know the Devil also speaks with "Forked Tongue," turning assertions into questions and lies into assertions all in an attempt to deceive. He makes up things just to serve his own ends. Believe me.

Now, in Medieval times, the lie was considered a "sin" and the sinfulness wasn't so much in the misuse of language (something Trump does masterfully), but in the liar's intention to deceive. By the 13th century, one thing was clear about lies: there were lies and there were women and every woman was thought to be a liar. But over time, things sorta shifted and the onus of lying, of deceiving became the wheelhouse of men since men were always adorning themselves in fine clothes to distract attention from their aging faces, sagging chins, graying hair and they dyed their beards and hair as a way to try deceiving old age. Today, one might use blue suits, red ties, white shirts, color one's hair and face orange. Sad. So, even in Pre-Trumpian days, men spent hours prepping their hair, powdering their faces, and scenting their bodies. It was thought, those things were merely artificial trappings of courage and valor and hid their true cowardly souls of rabbits or, maybe, turtles. By the beginning of the 18th century and because of the differences in wealth and status between the rich and the poor, it became necessary to appear to be something other than what one was. To be and to seem became two altogether different things and from this distraction came the rise of conspicuous ostentation, deceptive cunning and all the vices that come from them. Believe me.

It was the 18th century French philosopher, Rousseau who established the notion that because humans have become social, we value more what people think about us than what we really are and our lies have become more refined to reflect that need. To lie is to conceal a truth one ought to make manifest. By the end of the 18th century, lying and deception had become normalized. One might agree with the famous German philosopher Kant that when we lie, we violate the purpose of human communication which consists in the honest revelation of our thoughts to others.

If we can accept those things about lying and deception, then Donald Trump might be the biggest liar since the Devil perpetrated the Father of all Lies to that naïve girl in the garden. But perhaps there's a way we can use the lie to our benefit. To turn such deceit to our benefit. In other words, maybe there's a way we can learn how to…

Lie Like Trump.

A Lexicon of Trumpian Lies

*The trust of the innocent
is the liar's most useful tool.*

- STEPHEN KING

In no particular order, these are the types of lies Trump has managed to tell in his six decades of lying giving him the benefit of the doubt he began lying in earnest at the age of ten. These lies don't necessarily exist in a vacuum. In other words, they often cross over.

The Big Lie

This is better known as the **propaganda lie.** Though Hitler used it often, it was popularized by his Minister of Propaganda, Joseph Goebbels based on his quote, "The essential English leadership secret does not depend on particular intelligence. Rather, it depends on a remarkably stupid thick-headedness. The English follow the principle that when one lies, one should lie big, and stick to it. They keep up their lies, even at the risk of looking ridiculous." The Big Lie is a lie that turns the victimizer into the victim. This is a lie that Trump uses invariably to make himself the victim.

White Lie

One of the least offensive of lies, meant to spare someone's feelings. These don't really exist in the Trumposphere.

The Whopper or Pinocchio Lie

This lie is something unusually large or otherwise extreme of its kind; an extravagant or monstrous lie. The Whopper differs from The Big Lie in that it doesn't necessarily have a tragic or negative impact on anyone, but is meant for the liar to get something he wants.

Hyperbolic or Half-Truths

Distorts the truth, but falls short of an outright lie. This could also be called the *Cliff Clavin Lie* in which the liar exaggerates his intellect by combining bits of truth with fiction.

The Concealment Lie

A lie that leaves out something critical and relevant. Not unlike the *Cliff Clavin* lie with the difference being someone will invariably be hurt by it.

The Fib

An unimportant lie. Can also be called the **Throw Away Lie** since it's quickly forgotten.

Bullshit

Nonsense. In Trump's case, something like double talk.

Horseshit

Similar to bullshit, but with an attitude.

Double-Talk

Is a form of speech in which inappropriate, invented, or nonsense words are used to give the appearance of knowledge and so confuse or amuse an audience. Trump often resorts to this when he uses words such as "really" or "great" or any other superlative

related to the Bullshit he's saying.

Puffery

Exaggerated or false praise. This type of lie Trump reserves for lauding dictators such as Kim, Putin, Dutarte and any other autocrat he may ever meet.

Repetitious Lie

Also a fictitious lie similar to the alleged, Bowling Green Massacre.

Bald (Bold)-Face Lie

This is a lie everyone knows is a lie except the liar telling it since he's adamant about its veracity.

Deceptive Lie

Similar to the Half-Truth in that the liar leaves out much of the truth in order to make himself appear more impressive.

Duplicitous Lie

This is a lie spoken by liars who break their word. This could also be called the Tartuffe Lie in which the liar knows he's lying, but tells people what they want to hear because they trust him.

Compulsive or Pathological Lie

Is the lie the liar tells and continues to tell because it's based on his own fabricated "facts."

Fake News

In a post-truth world, fake news is what pre-post truth writers would call fiction, but in a Trump world it becomes…

Lie Like

Trump

A lie told often enough becomes the truth.

- Vladimir Lenin

No man lies so boldly as the man who is indignant.

- Friedrich Nietzsche

A Christian Situation:

When asked why you don't go to church on Easter or any other religious holiday to celebrate your Lord and Savior, Jesus Christ...

Lie Like Trump...

"I like people that weren't
CAPTURED

...Okay?"

Family Leadership Summit,
Ames, Iowa,
July 18, 2015

An Awkward Situation:

Your son is going on his first date with a girl he knows from church. He asks you for some advice on what to do when he drives her home and walks her to the door and there's an awkward moment...

Lie Like Trump...

"I just start

kissing them.

It's like a magnet."

- Trump
Billy Bush Interview
Access Hollywood, 2005

A Very Awkward Situation:

Your son is going to the high school prom with his first girlfriend. He asks you for some advice on what to do if she won't give him a kiss goodnight…

Lie Like Trump…

"Grab'em by the

PUSSY.

You can do anything."

- Trump
Billy Bush Interview,
Access Hollywood, 2005

A Latino Situation:

You take your family to Disneyland as a birthday present for your 5-year old daughter. While waiting in line, you see a Latino family of eight ahead of you and it takes a while for them all to get through the line. Throwing a temper tantrum, your daughter asks why it's taking so long…

Lie Like Trump…

"Chain MIGRATION must end now!"

- Trump
Twitter
November 7, 2017

An Environmental Situation:

There are only two of you in an elevator and after a heavy Mexican lunch of chilies and black beans, you pass a hazardous fart. Instead of apologizing…

Lie Like Trump…

"Well...China will be able to increase these

emissions

by a staggering number of years."

- Trump
Paris Climate Accord
June 1, 2017

A Classroom Situation:

In your world history class, you have to give an oral report on the Nazi atrocities. Instead of studying the history books for your report, you played golf instead and when it comes time for the report...

Lie Like Trump...

"You had a group on one side that was

bad

and you had a group on the other side that was also very violent."

- Trump
After Charlottesville
News Conference in New
York, 2017

A Bizarre Situation:

You are on trial for a brutal murder. You are asked by the prosecutor to try on a pair of black leather gloves allegedly used during the crime to see if they fit. While pretending the gloves don't fit…

Lie Like Trump…

"My **fingers** are

long and beautiful,

as... it has been
well documented,
are various other
parts
of my body."

- Trump
New York Post, 2011

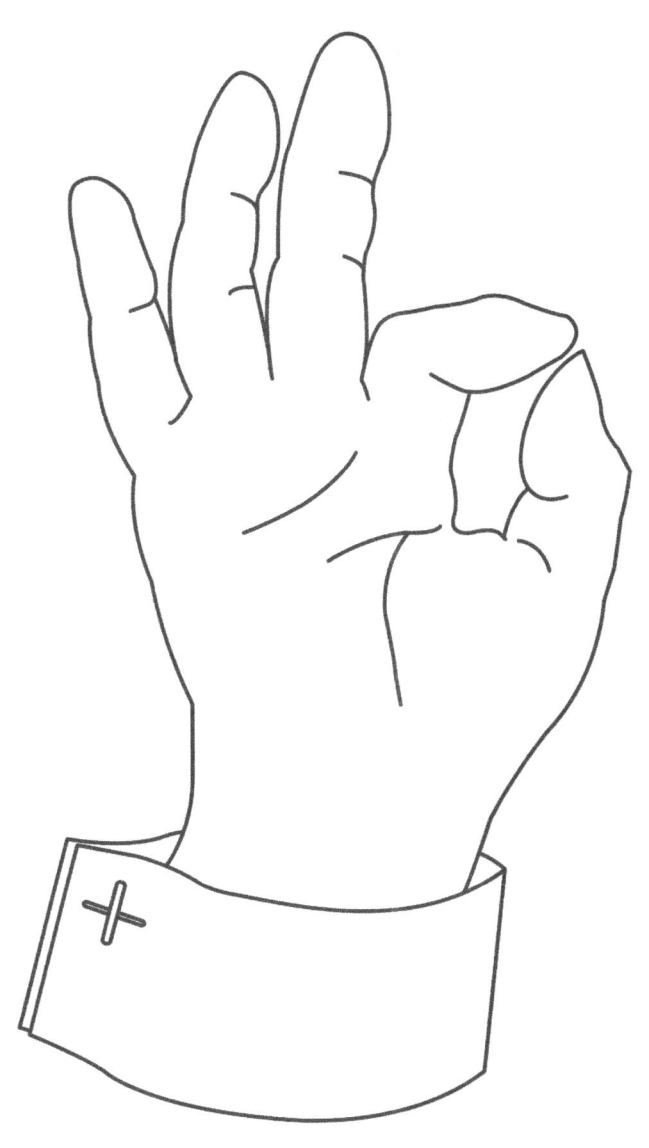

"I play to people's fantasies."

- Trump: The Art of the Deal, 1987

Marge, it takes two to lie;
one to lie and one to listen.

- Homer Simpson

A College Situation:

It's your senior year of college and you're taking a course in the rise of the women's suffrage and women's rights movements in the United States. When asked how you feel about the movements and whether they have made major gains over the decades…

Lie Like Trump…

"I don't want to sound too much like a **chauvinist**, but when I come home and dinner's not ready, I'll go through the

roof!

...okay?"

- Trump
ABC's Primetime Live
1994

An Unusual Situation:

You've done very little volunteer work in your life, but because a friend of yours is ill, he's asked you to sub for him and give a speech at the *Special Olympics*. Unfortunately, you really didn't make any effort at preparing a speech and having nothing to read, you…

Lie Like Trump…

"Sorry losers and haters, but my I.Q. is one of the highest, and you all know it. Please don't feel so stupid or insecure, it's not your fault."

- Trump
Twitter
May 8, 2013

A Christian Situation:

You are in the confessional booth and the Father asks you to name your sins and tell how many times you've committed each one since only by confessing will you enter the gates of heaven…

Lie Like Trump…

"I consider myself too **perfect** And Have No faults."

- Trump
Twitter
January 13, 2014

42

A Marital Situation:

You and your wife have been attending marital counseling and have been asked to keep a journal for the sessions, which you think is a stupid idea. At your next session, the counselor askes you how your journal is going…

Lie Like Trump…

"If I told the

real

stories

of my experiences with women, often seemingly very happily married and important women, my book would be a best seller."

- Trump
The Art of the Comeback
1997

An Awkward Situation:

You are in the confessional booth and the Father, leaning closer, asks if you could repeat your confession since he didn't hear it quite well the first time. Not really interested in his answer, you..

Lie Like Trump...

"Do you mind if I sit back a little? Because your breath is very

bad,

...it really is."

- Trump
Larry King
April 15, 1989

46

A Romantic Situation:

A friend set you up on a blind date with a very unattractive person. Your date says that she is a little uncomfortable going on blind dates and asks you how you feel about them…

Lie Like Trump…

"I feel like a supermodel, except, like, times 10, okay? It's true. I'm a

SUPERMODEL"

- Trump
Speech in Arizona
June 18, 2016

A Professional Situation:

After many successful years in the corporate world, you've been short-listed for a job with the Trump administration. The first question you're asked at the interview is why you would be the best candidate for the job…

Lie Like Trump…

"I have a good
brain and
I've said a lot
of things."

- Trump
MSNBC Morning Joe
March 16, 2016

A Religious Situation:

Your partner demands that you go to church with her. "You might just learn something," she says. You are bored out of your mind when the pastor begins to read from the Bible, John 1:1...*In the beginning was the Word, and the Word was with God, and the Word was God.*

Unimpressed, you turn to your partner and...

Lie Like Trump...

"i KNOW WORDS. i HAVE THE BEST WORDS."

- Trump
Campaign rally
December 30, 2015

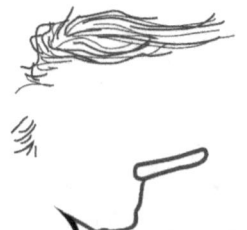

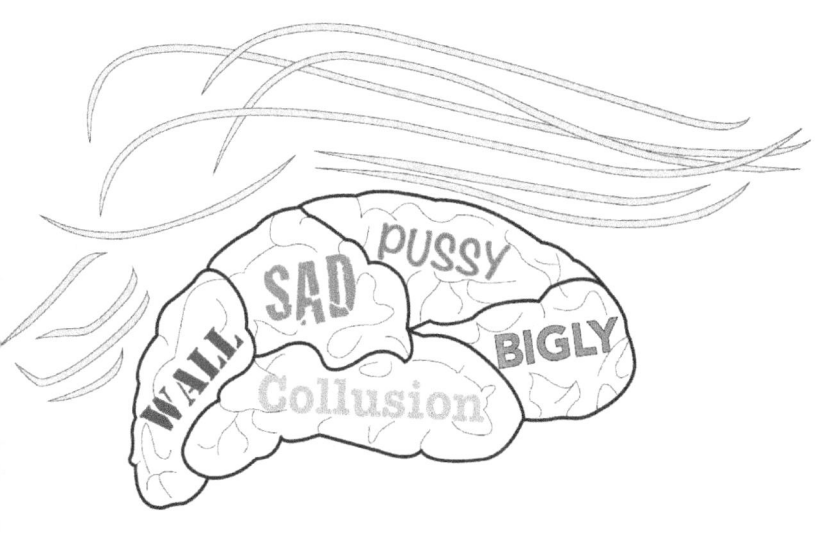

People who boast about
their IQ are losers.

- Stephen Hawking

An Awkward Situation:

You are volunteering as a camp counselor when your supervisor walks in and asks you if you've read the morning papers about the latest D.C. sex scandal…

Lie Like Trump…

"You know, it really doesn't matter what the media writes as long as you've got a

young

and

beautiful

piece of **ASS**."

- Trump
Esquire magazine, 1991

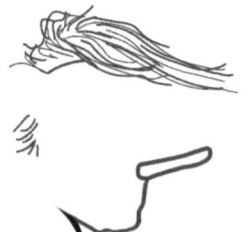

A Financial Situation:

A group of girl scouts are at your door selling cookies. After paying cash for a few boxes, your wife brings it to your attention that the girls gave you back too much change. Instead of giving the money back…

Lie Like Trump…

"The point is, you can never be too

GREEDY."

- Trump
The Art of the Deal, 1987

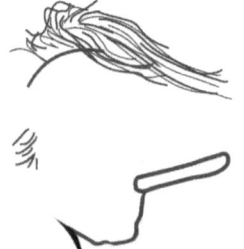

An In-law Situation:

You've been married for 20 years and have never celebrated your mother-in-law's birthday. Your wife asks why you never want to go visit her, and asks "What's the problem?"

Lie Like Trump...

"Crude, rude, obnoxious and

dumb – other

than that I like her very much."

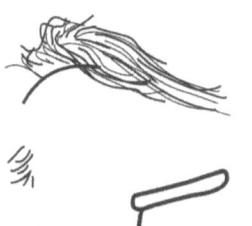

- Trump
Twitter
July 11, 2014

An Awkward Situation:

Your daughter comes home from grade school and tells you they are learning all about sex education. She asks you to help explain what it is…

Lie Like Trump…

"It's so

nasty

though,...ugh,

I'm so good."

- Trump
Sioux Center, Iowa
January 23, 2016

A Birthday Situation:

Your wife just gave birth to a beautiful baby girl. It's your first child and your wife is overjoyed. The nurse's aide asks you what you think of having such a beautiful daughter…

Lie Like Trump…

"A person who is very **flat-chested** is very hard to be a **10.**"

- Trump
Howard Stern interview
2005

An Inspirational Situation:

While visiting the Missionaries of Charity in Calcutta, founded by Mother Teresa, one of the nuns asks you what inspired you to make the long pilgrimage from the United States to Calcutta…

Lie Like Trump…

"Any girl

you have I can take
from you."

- Trump
Howard Stern interview
2001

A Penile Situation:

You are buying a box of condoms and a box of male enhancement pills at your local pharmacy when the cute cashier asks you if you need anything else...

Lie Like Trump...

"Frankly, I wouldn't mind if there were an anti-Viagra, something with the opposite effect. I'm not BRAGGING."

- Trump
Playboy interview
2004

A Childish Situation:

Your eight-year old child did not study for a math test and comes home with a failing grade. Before he shows you the grade, he sees a copy of **"Lie Like Trump"** on your desk and reads it...

Your child Lies Like Trump...

"It's a **rigged** deal folks. It's a **rigged** deal. I used to say it. It's a **rigged** deal. It's a disgrace."

- Trump
Rally, July 5, 2018

A Christmas Situation:

Your 6 year old son was given a brand new improved Lego set for Christmas by his Mexican nanny, Margarita. After unwrapping the present, he asks you if you can help him build a wall like they have in China…

Lie Like Trump…

"I will build a Great

and nobody builds walls better than

me,

...believe me."

- Trump
Campaign announcement
June 16, 2015

73

Stop telling outlandish lies,
Stop turning minnows into whales.

- Dr. Seuss

An Awkward Situation:

While discussing the state of geopolitical affairs about Israel, you are asked about your opinion of Isaiah 45:17 that states Israel can only be saved by the **LORD** with an everlasting salvation…

Lie Like Trump…

"Nobody but Donald Trump will save Israel."

- Trump
Twitter
April 27, 2015

A Scary Situation:

You are running late for a Halloween party so you stop at the local party store and decide to buy the traditional white sheet ghost costume. The store is very busy and to expedite things you put on the sheet and start to exit the store without paying when the alarm sounds. You're stopped by security guards...

Lie Like Trump...

"Look at my African American over there. ...Look at him!"

- Trump
Redding's Airport, CA.
June 3, 2016

A Dinner Situation:

Your wife wants to go to the opening of an exclusive Mexican restaurant for dinner, but you say you'd rather not go. When she asks you why…

Lie Like Trump:…

"They're bringing **drugs**.
They're bringing **crime**.
They're

rapists."

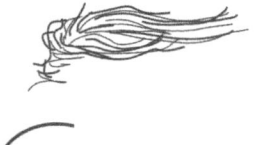

- Trump
Campaign Announcement,
June, 2015

An Asian Situation:

After a huge Chinese dinner of spring rolls, satay chicken and spare ribs, you're asked to read your fortune cookie. It actually reads, "Woman run faster with skirt up than man with pants down." Feeling confused you…

Lie Like Trump..

"We can't continue to allow **CHINA** to

RAPE our country...

and that's what
they're doing."

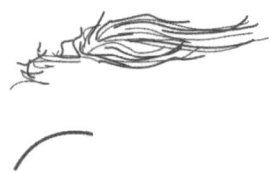

-Trump
Fort Wayne, Indiana
May 1, 2016

An Environmental Situation:

The weather has been blistering, breaking all records and your wife is pleading with you to turn on the air conditioner. Not wanting to spend the money…

Lie Like Trump…

"The concept of

global warming was

created by and for the

Chinese…"

- Trump
Twitter
November 6, 2012

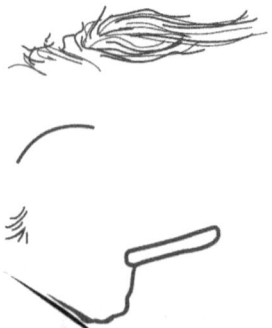

84

A Family Situation:

At the dinner table, the conversation turns to women's issues like contraception and abortion. Your daughter is pro-choice and your son is pro-life. Knowing they look to you for Fatherly advice, they ask where you stand on the issue…

Lie Like Trump…

"Right.

I'm pro-choice...

I'm pro-life...

I'm sorry."

- Trump
CNN Jake Tapper
June 28, 2015

A Family Situation (cont.):

Still at the dinner table, your children are not going to let you off the hook and demand you take a stand on the issue, one way or the other. Since riding the fence is not an option for you…

Lie Like Trump…

"I don't stand by

anything."

- Trump
CBS News
John Dickerson, 2017

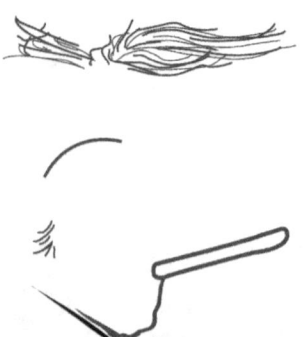

A Commitment Situation:

While making your vows at your wedding, the Minister asks you if you will take this woman to have and to hold, from this day forward, for better, for worse, for richer, for poorer, in sickness and in health, to love and to cherish, 'til death do you part…You think for a moment and then…

Lie Like Trump…

"**WHat tHe HeLL do I KNoW? I've beeN**

DIVORCED

tWice."

- Trump
Think Big, 2007

A Family Situation:

While vacationing in Hawaii with your 8 year old daughter, she tells you she learned in science class the islands are part of an archipelago, but asks you what you know about the islands. Dumbfounded…you…

Lie Like Trump..

"THIS is AN isLANd, surroundEd BY WATER, Big WATER, OCEAN WATER."

- Trump
Disaster relief effort
for Puerto Rico
September 2017

A Jewish Situation:

It's tax season and one of your colleagues, who's been audited in the past, is looking for a new accountant since the last one didn't save him any money. He asks you if you have any suggestions and you…

Lie Like Trump…

"The only kind of people I want counting my $MONEY are short guys that wear yarmulkes every day."

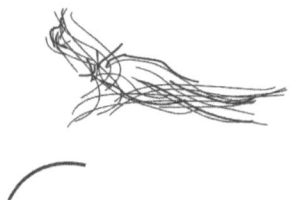

Trumped! 1991,
Simon & Schuster

94

An Anthony Weiner Situation:

Your wife catches you in the act of **sexting** on your phone with strange women who are sending you nude pictures and erotic sexual messages. Enraged she confronts you…

Lie Like Trump…

"Just remember, what
you are seeing and
what you are reading

is **not** what's

happening."

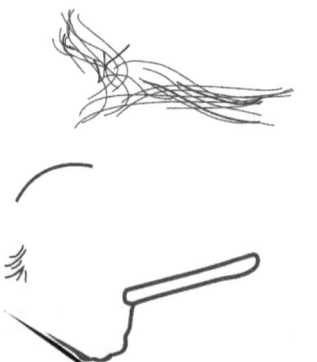

- Trump
Kansas City
July 24, 2018

A Religious Situation:

Someone asks you if you believe in the *Immaculate Conception*. Not being a very religious person, but not wanting to look ignorant, you…

Lie Like Trump…

"I believe in clean air.

Immaculate

air."

- Trump
CNN
September 24, 2015

An International Situation:

You're studying for your SAT exam and your tutor asks you to talk about what you know about Europe and European history. Not sure how to answer…you ponder the question then…

Lie Like Trump…

"Europe is a **big** place."

- Trump
The O'Reilly Factor
March 31, 2016

An Awkward Situation:

You've been nominated by your son's school to be president of the PTA association. You wear your favorite sport coat, but fail to zip up your fly. When your son calls that to your attention, only moments before you're about to speak, you...

Lie Like Trump...

Do I look like a president? How **handsome** am I, right?

How

handsome?

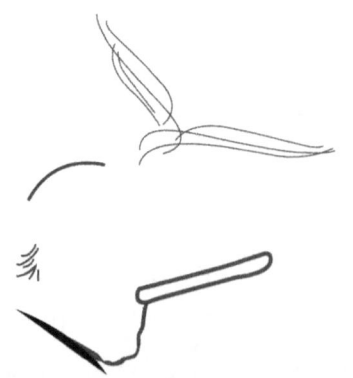

- Trump
April 25, 2016

A Religious Situation:

While visiting a cathedral in Italy with your wife, you come upon a magnificent stained glass window of Mary Magdalene washing the feet of **Jesus**. Your wife asks you what you think about such a beautiful piece of art…

Lie Like Trump:

"Women: you have to treat'em like shit."

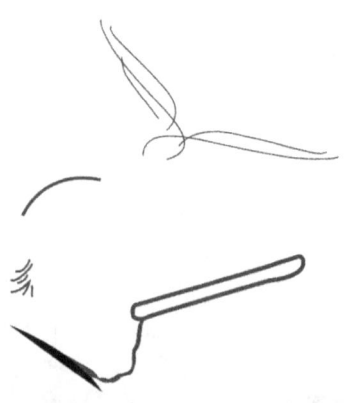

- Trump
New York magazine
November 9, 1992

A Ballistic Situation:

You are the President of the United States and you have just been notified of an incoming ballistic missile attack while you are tweeting on the toilet. Anxiously, your top general asks you twice, what will you do…what will you do?...

Lie Like Trump…

"My Attention Span is short."

- Trump
Surviving at the top, 1990

An Apocalyptic Situation:

You are at your court ordered anger management session with your therapist because of your explosive tweets. She wants to blast a barrage of insults at you to watch your responses, reminding you of the teaching of **Jesus** to *turn the other cheek.*
Instead you…

Lie Like Trump…

"WHY CAN'T WE USE NUCLEAR WEAPONS?"

- Trump
MSNBC
August 3, 2016

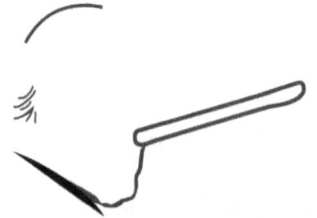

Speed Lying

No one reads the Bible more than me Nobody's ever been more successful than me Nobody has better toys than I do Nobody is stronger than me Nobody is bigger or better at the military than I am Nobody loves the Bible more than I do Nobody builds walls better than me Nobody's better to people with disabilities than me There's nobody more pro-Israel than I am I'm really good at war I know more about ISIS than the generals do There is no one who respects women more than I do Nobody knows more about trade than me Nobody knows the game better than me I was always the best athlete Nobody knows banking better than I do I understand money better than anybody Nobody knows politicians better than I do Nobody knows more about debt

than I do Nobody knows the system
better than me I'm the best
builder I know more about wedges
than any human being that's lived
I'm the strongest person on the
Second Amendment that exists I
have one of the great
temperaments Nobody can do it
like me I give myself a 10 out of
10 I'm a very stable genius My IQ
is one of the highest I Have the
best words Nobody knows more
about taxes than I do People
would say I'm the super genius of
all time I consider myself too
perfect I know more about
renewables than any human being
on Earth I have greater patience
than any human being in the world
I can be more presidential than
anybody I'm the greatest person

**Nobody is better on humility than
me.**

- Donald Trump

BREAKING NEWS!

The White House wants to clarify the phrase, "Enemy of the people." What Mr. Trump meant to say was, "Enemas for the people" related to many Americans who suffer from one kind of intestinal ailment or another. Mr. Trump who also has had bouts of intestinal disorders based on his diet, felt a kind of empathy for his fellow Americans who suffer from the same thing. When asked about the clarification, White House intestinologist, Sarah Sanders said, "As usual, the media can't hear things Mr. Trump says. You should all go back and review the tapes. He clearly says, 'Enemas for the people,' but as usual none of you can hear let alone write." When one reporter asked why enemas instead of an anti-acid, Sanders was quick to bark, "Always something anti. Anti-Russia, anti-tariff, anti-abortion, anti-immigration, anti-acid. If he didn't say you were 'Enemies of the people" instead of 'enemas' he should have!" There were no more questions however, some reporters were handing out Rolaids to anyone who wanted one.

BREAKING NEWS!

Taking a recommendation from Rush Limbaugh, Mr. Trump has suggested that all K-12 schools throughout the United States install AR-15 cabinets similar to those used for fire extinguishers in all classrooms. The cabinets themselves would cost $150 each (much less with the volume purchased) and the AR-15s would run about $600 that would be $750 for each classroom and each administrative office in each school times the number of schools in the United States. The Office of Budget Management estimates the cost for doing this in every classroom in every K-12 school in the United States would be around $1Billion. When Limbaugh was asked who would pay for that he suggested "the schools themselves including teachers and students." When he was told that most schools don't have enough money for pencils and paper let alone AR-15s Limbaugh opined, "They have to make choices." When asked if he concurred with the always-insightful Limbaugh, Mr. Trump replied that since "almost every single one of these crimes have been committed by Latinos, Mexico will pay for it." Mexican President Enrique Peña Nieto was unavailable for comment, but former President Vicente Fox was quoted as saying "The moron can go fuck himself."

BREAKING NEWS!

World Renowned Entrepreneur & MORTALITY Loser

Donald Trump PASSES AWAY!

June 14, 1946 – July 4, 2020

After a lengthy battle with a rare and untreatable human form of hoof-and-mouth disease, Mr. Trump, aged 74, died agitatedly on July 4 at the Mayo Clinic in Rochester, Minnesota. Known primarily as an entrepreneur and staunch advocate of insulting anyone who didn't agree with him as well as being only the second US president forced to resign, Trump inherited a vast fortune from his father and proceeded to make an even vaster fortune based on those good graces of his father. A native of Queens, Trump attended Fordham University for two years before transferring to the Wharton School of Economics where he graduated in 1968 with a Bachelor of Science degree in economics and anthropology. Contrary to what he said in life, in death he had no advanced degrees.

After completing his undergraduate degree, Mr. Trump avoided the Vietnam War by receiving multiple deferments based on an alleged "bone spur" in one of his feet, though the exact foot he could not remember. He then went on to begin a highly lucrative real estate career funded primarily by his father. By 1989, poor business decisions left Trump unable to meet loan payments. Trump financed the construction of his third casino, the $1 billion Taj Mahal, primarily with high-interest junk bonds. Although he shored up his businesses with additional loans and postponed interest payments, by 1991, increasing debt brought Trump to business bankruptcy and to the brink of personal bankruptcy.

Known primarily for his presidential runs, both real and imagined, beginning in 2008, he won the 2016 Republican nomination for president and secured his presidency even though losing the popular vote by an estimated 3 million votes. At his inauguration speech, Trump graciously called Ms. Clinton, "The biggest ho' in America and will be jailed on my first full day in office." When asked what he wanted his legacy to be, Trump said, "That I'm smart, really, really smart and rich, really, really rich."

Funeral arrangements are being handled by Solipsistic Funeral Home in the Bronx. The funeral will be held at 11:30 am on Wednesday, July 5th at the funeral home; burial will follow at Sweet Passages Cemetery. In lieu of flowers, the family asks that you consider donations to the Donald Trump Fund for the Treatment of Bellicosity. It is estimated that the funeral attendance will be the largest since the parade down Fifth Avenue at the end of World War II.

CROSS MY HEART

& HOPE TO DIE

In case you forgot the poem, it goes like this:

Cross my heart and hope to die

Stick a needle in my eye

Wait a moment; I spoke a lie

I never really wanted to die.

But if I may and if I might

My heart is open for tonight

Though my lips are sealed and a promise is true

I won't break my word, my word to you.

The origins of the poem are sketchy, but it wouldn't be surprising to hear Trump declare he wrote it himself when he was knee high to a Nebraska cornstalk in July. It's not going out on a limb to propose Donald Trump is and has always been a pathological liar. In some ways, he must be proud of that since he's been doing it for decades. Perhaps, they gave out Boy Scout Merit Badges for lying at one time and he received the first one. There's not much to conclude here except by saying, perhaps, at future Presidential inaugurations, the Chief Justice of the Supreme Court (assuming there is a Supreme Court) should recite the above poem and have the President repeat it along with the Presidential Oath which goes something like this:

I do solemnly swear (or affirm) that I will faithfully execute the office of President of the United States, and will to the best of my ability, preserve, protect and defend the Constitution of the United States.

If one consults Chapter Three, A Lexicon of Trumpian Lies, this particular lie might fall under the category of, "The Biggest Lie" since if pathological lying is a President's way of preserving, protecting and defending the Constitution of the United States, then may God have mercy on us all.

About the Authors

Half the lies they tell about us aren't true.

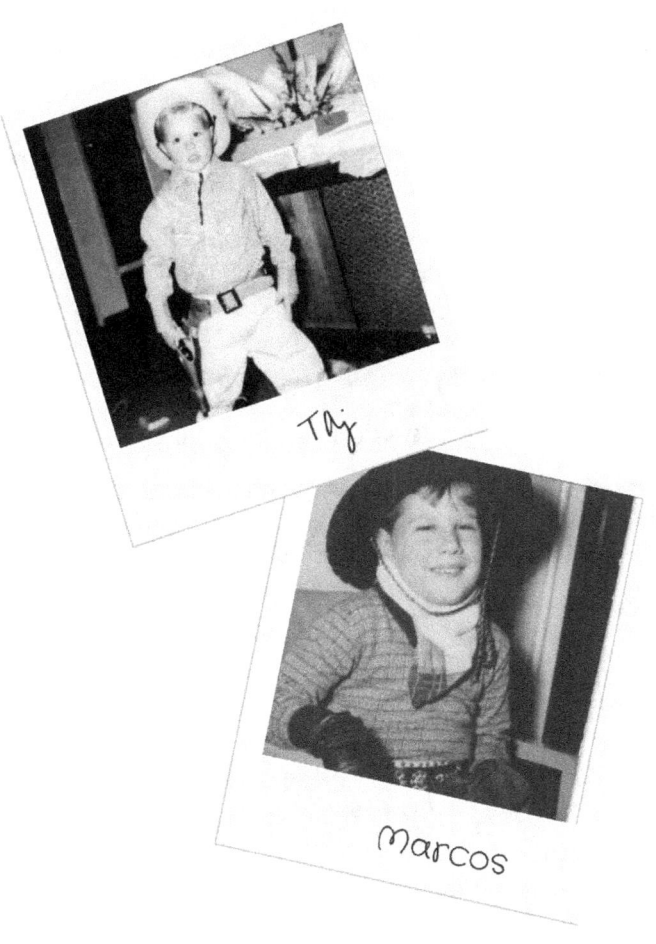

Taj

Marcos

Taj Mahal was named after the failed *Trump Taj Mahal* casino in Atlantic City, known as the first casino with a strip club. Unable to afford care for little Taj on her pitiful wages as an emigrant cocktail hostess at the casino, his mother left him with a Christian couple that performed instant weddings for losers. The next day, after receiving a mysterious check for $150,000, his mother left for Slovenia. Sad. Today, Taj runs a televangelical empire using a pseudonym and travels the world in his private gold jet (aka God's Chariot) saving those same losers from worldly vices while making an ungodly amount of money. He is currently developing the first Casino for God where everyone is a winner because all losses are considered a religious charitable deduction.

Marcos Ejevarilla was born in Buenos Aires, Argentina. After finishing high school at the prestigious Macedonio Fernandez School of Fine Arts, he and his family immigrated to Mexico. Ejevarilla won a full scholarship to Exeter College, Oxford where he graduated with honors in 20th century Latin American Literature. He returned to the United States and began a PhD in Ecumenical Narrative Fiction at Harvard where he also graduated with honors and upon leaving Harvard, began another PhD in Solipsistic Political Theory at Yale. Unfortunately, Ejevarilla has become overqualified for too many jobs and unable to find decent minimum wage work, he presently parks cars at Le Diplomate restaurant in D.C. He's considering a law degree at Georgetown if *Lie Like Trump* makes him enough money for tuition and for paying legal expenses to get his family out of a Texas concentration camp.

Works Consulted

Oxford English Dictionary. Oxford: Oxford University Press.

Acontius. *Satan's Strategies.*

Denery II, Dallas G. *The Devil Wins: A History of Lying from the Garden of Eden to the Enlightenment.* Princeton, NJ: Princeton University Press, Date 2015

Goodreads.com/quotes/tag/lying

St. Augustine. *Against Lying.*

Scott, Gini Graham. *Playing the Lying Game: detecting and dealing with lies and liars from occasional fibbers to frequent fabricators.* Santa Barbara, CA: Praeger Press, 2010.

www.washingtonpost.com

www.edition.cnn.com

www.fnietzsche.com

www.minnpost.com

www.wikipedia.com